Special Message

_____

_____

_____

_____

_____

_____

With Love, _____

Stick your favorite
picture here

Charlie

is surrounded with so much love.

You may even think it comes from above.

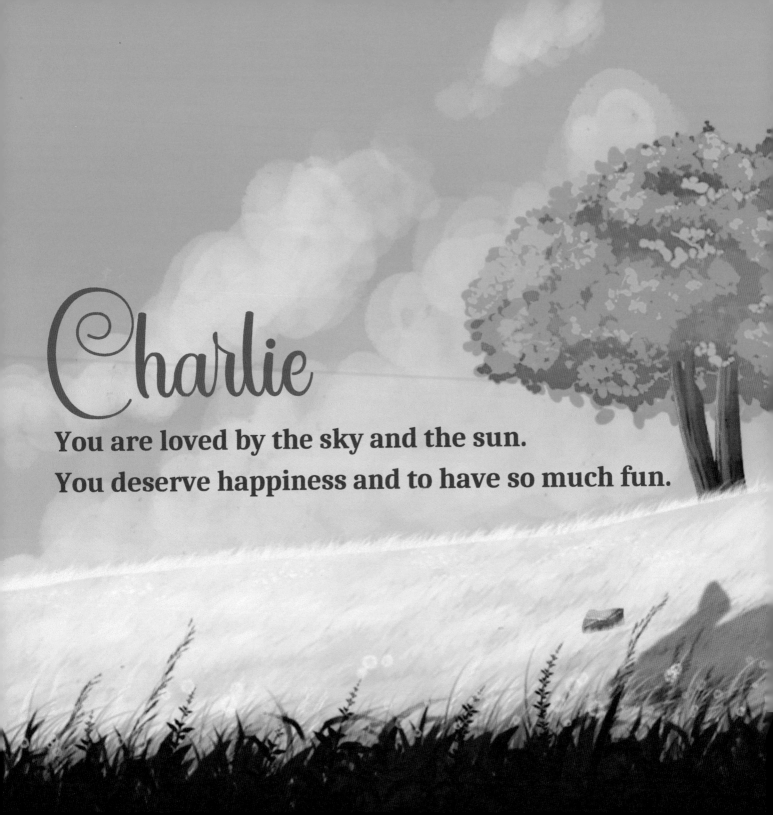

Charlie

You are loved by the sky and the sun.

You deserve happiness and to have so much fun.

Charlie

You are loved by the trees and the leaves that fall.

You are loved by everyone and all.

Charlie

You are loved by the wind and the breeze.
You deserve the best hugging squeeze.

Charlie

You are loved by the birds that tweet.
All because you are so gentle and sweet.

Charlie

You are loved by the flowers
in the ground.
There is so much love all around.

Charlie

You are loved by the moon and night.
You shine like the stars with the brightest light.

Charlie

You are loved with your beautiful heart.
You are beautiful, amazing, and oh so smart.

Charlie

You are loved from head to toes.
You are loved by your family so close.

Merry Christmas.
Love, Grandma

Your Uncle
loves you!
Merry Christmas

From
ntie

Charlie

You will be loved for the rest of your days.
You will be loved forever and always.

The end

34300671R00016